REGINALD GOES TO THE FAIR

WRITTEN BY
KATHERINE RAWSON

ILLUSTRATED BY
MAX STASIUK

PIONEER VALLEY EDUCATIONAL PRESS, INC.

CONTENTS

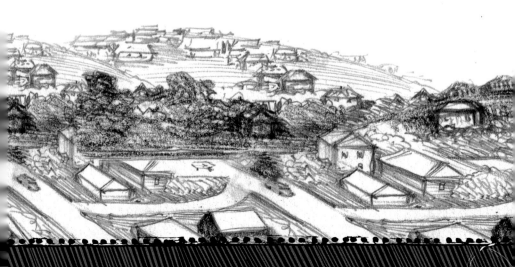

CHAPTER 1
A BUSY MORNING

It was a busy summer morning at Reginald's house. Amy and Jack were helping their parents clean the house. They were washing and dusting and vacuuming. They were picking things up and putting them away.

They were too busy to pay attention to Reginald.

Reginald stuck his head
through the kitchen door
to see what Amy was doing.

"You can't come in here,"
said Amy. "We just finished
washing the floor."

Next, Reginald wandered
into the living room to see
what Jack was doing.

"You can't come in here,"
said Jack. "I'm busy vacuuming."

"Amy, put Reginald outside,"
said her father. "He can't be
in the house while we're cleaning."

Amy opened the front door.
"Go outside, Reginald," she said.
"We'll come out later to play
with you."

Reginald stood in the front
yard and looked around.
There were no squirrels to chase.
There were no bones to chew.
There were no soccer balls to kick.

There was nothing to do
and no one to play with.
Reginald felt sad and lonely.

There was nothing to do in the yard,
so Reginald wandered out
to the sidewalk to see what was
happening in the neighborhood.
He trotted down the street,
watching the cars whoosh past him.

Reginald walked for blocks
and blocks. After a while,
he noticed the cars weren't whooshing
anymore. They were moving
very slowly in a long line.

Up ahead, the cars were driving through an open gate. He noticed a big sign that said:
COUNTY FAIR THIS WEEKEND.

Reginald walked through
the gate. He walked past a booth with a sign that said:
ENTRANCE: $10 PER CAR.

All the drivers stopped at the booth and handed money to the woman inside. Reginald walked right past the booth. He couldn't read the signs, and he didn't have any money, anyway.

CHAPTER 2
AT THE FAIR

Reginald wandered through
the fairgrounds, watching the crowds
of people.

A man walked by with a hot
dog dripping bright yellow mustard.
"Mmmm! What a delicious smell,"
thought Reginald. He followed
the man.

Then he noticed a girl carrying
a huge mound of pink cotton candy
in a paper cone. "Mmmm! How
tasty that looks," thought Reginald.
He started walking behind the girl.

Next, he spied a group of children
eating popcorn out of a bag.
"Mmmm! Salty!" Reginald
trotted towards the children.

There were so many delicious smells
in the air, Reginald didn't know
what to look at or where to go.

Then, he smelled a very
different kind of smell. He stopped
to sniff. This was something extra
special. He smelled straw and
sweat and hooves and barns.
It smelled like farm animals!

Reginald loved farm animals.
He loved everything about them —
the smells, the straw, and
the sounds of all the animals.

He followed the special smell
through the crowd, until he came
to a long, low building. His ears
perked up. He could hear
the sounds of *moo's* and *neigh's*
and *baa's* and *oink's* coming
from inside the building.

He stepped through the doorway.
Inside, it was dark and warm.
Reginald stood quietly and
sniffed deeply.

A soft *moo* came
from behind him. He turned and
saw a calf standing in a stall, with
a blue ribbon hung on the wall.

"Woof!" Reginald greeted the calf. He saw something in front of the stall. "Straw!" he thought.

With a joyful yelp, he jumped into the huge pile of straw. He rolled and rolled. Then he lay on his back and wiggled around. How good it felt! He stood up, shaking the straw off his fur, and continued walking through the building.

Reginald passed stalls full of sheep. He passed stalls full of horses.

"*Baa!*" bleated the sheep, staring at Reginald.

"*Neigh!*" said the horses,
  and they stamped their hooves.

"Woof!" Reginald answered back.

Reginald heard grunting and
snorting. He came to a large pen.
Pigs were wallowing around in a
big puddle of mud. "Mud!" thought
Reginald.

Mud!

"*Oink! Oink! Oink!*" squealed
the pigs.

"Mud!" Reginald thought happily.
He squeezed under the fence
and plunged into the mud
with the pigs. He rolled and rolled
and rolled and rolled until he was
covered with a thick layer
of stinky, gooey mud.

"I love mud!" thought Reginald
as he stood up and shook
off some loose mud.

"Woof!" he barked goodbye
to the pigs. Then he squeezed back
under the fence and out the back
entrance of the barn. Outside,
the sun was bright and hot,
and the mud on Reginald's fur
dried quickly.

CHAPTER 3
THE PIE CONTEST

Reginald was coated with dried mud from the top of his head to the tip of his tail. He was also covered with small bits of straw and a very strong stench from the barn.

Reginald continued wandering through the fairgrounds. He saw a small building with a large sign by the door that read:
PIE CONTEST TODAY.

He couldn't read the sign, but he could smell delicious aromas drifting through the open door.

Reginald followed the delicious smells through the door and into another room. He saw several large tables, and each one was covered with rows of pies. There were apple, blueberry, lemon, and strawberry pies. There were custard, chocolate, and banana cream pies.

Reginald had never seen
so many pies in one place.
He started to drool. Several people, each wearing a badge that said, "Judge," were tasting the pies and making comments.

"Mmmm, delicious," one judge
said, her mouth full of lemon pie.

"Yes, very tasty," agreed another
gentleman, wiping crumbs
from his lips.

Reginald started walking toward the yummy-smelling pies. The judges all turned and stared.

"What is that awful stench?"

"Ewwwww, disgusting!"

"Unbearable!"

The judges hurried out the back entrance, gasping for fresh air.

Reginald jumped up on the nearest table and eyed the rows of pies. Then he began to eat.

CHAPTER 4
REGINALD RIDES

Reginald wandered outside
with a belly full of pie and a blob
of whipped cream on his nose.

He heard music playing in the
distance. "A merry-go-round!"
he thought. He had always wanted
to ride on one. As he ran toward
the music, the people scurried away.

"What a stench!"

"Terrible stink!"

"Awful!"

As Reginald trotted toward
the merry-go-round, he saw
several children waiting for a turn
to ride. He waited at the end
of the line.

"What's that nasty smell?"

"Sti-i-i-i-i-i-nky!"

"It's that smelly dog over there!"

The children turned to stare
at Reginald, then pinched
their noses and ran away.

When the merry-go-round stopped, the riders jumped off. They all ran away, pinching their noses and complaining about the awful stink.

Reginald had the merry-go-round all to himself! He jumped on, and it began to move — slowly at first, then faster and faster. Reginald felt the breeze on his face. His ears flapped out behind him. "What fun!" he thought.

When the ride stopped,
Reginald jumped off.
He heard a new sound nearby.
"Clickety-clack! Clickety-clack!"

"A roller coaster!" Reginald thought.
He had never been on one before.
He ran over and stood waiting
at the end of the line of people.

"Stinky!" everyone cried.
They dropped their tickets and fled.
When the roller coaster stopped,
the riders jumped off and ran away,
crying, "Stinky! Awful stench! Nasty!"

Reginald jumped into
the roller coaster's front car.

"Clickety-clack! Clickety-clack!"
Up, up, up it went, up the first hill.
"Woooooooof!" Reginald barked
as the roller coaster flew down
the other side of the hill.
Up and down and around
Reginald went. He had never
had so much fun in his life!

Next, he spied a huge wheel
in the sky. "A Ferris wheel!"
Reginald thought.

CHAPTER 5
AT THE TOP OF THE WORLD

Reginald scampered over to the Ferris wheel. The people in line dropped their tickets as the stinky, muddy dog approached. When the Ferris wheel stopped, all the riders jumped from their seats and hurried away, too.

Reginald didn't care, because now he had the Ferris wheel all to himself. He jumped into a seat, and the wheel began to move up, up, up, higher and higher.

Up, up, up he went!

As Reginald looked down, everything looked small and far away. He saw a line of cars driving out through the open gate.
"Where are all the people going?" Reginald wondered. He could hear faint cries below.

"Stinky!"

"Nasty!"

"Get me away from that awful smell!"

Reginald could see past the
fairgrounds to the houses beyond.
Far in the distance, he thought
he could see his own street
and his own house. He thought
about Amy and Jack.
Maybe they were looking for him!

Down, down, down went the
Ferris wheel. When Reginald reached
the bottom, he jumped out of the
seat and began to run. He raced
through the empty fairgrounds
and headed for home. Reginald didn't
notice the big black clouds
in the sky. He ran and ran, thinking
only about Amy and Jack.

A heavy drop of rain fell
from the sky and landed on his nose.
Reginald kept running. Another
drop fell, and then another. Soon
it was raining hard.

As Reginald ran toward home,
the rain began to wash the mud
and straw from his fur. By the time
he got to his own street, the rain
had stopped, and his fur was clean.
The stink had washed away, too!
He was a shiny, clean, sweet-smelling
dog once again.

Reginald ran up the front steps
of his house and scratched
at the door.

CHAPTER 6
BACK TO THE FAIR

"Reginald's back!"
cried Jack as he opened the door.

"Reginald!" shouted Amy,
hugging him tight.

"Don't let that dirty dog in this
clean house," said their father.

"He's not dirty," said Jack.
"He's beautiful and clean."

"Can we take Reginald
to the fair with us? Please?"
pleaded Amy.

"All right. Go get his leash,"
said their father.

Reginald sat in the back seat with Amy and Jack. "You'll love the fair, Reginald," said Amy.

"We worked hard all day
   cleaning the house," explained Jack.
"Now we get to go to the fair!"

They drove to the fair, parked
the car, and walked to the county
fair entrance.

"I'm sorry," said the woman in the booth, "but your dog can not come into the fair."

"Please," said Jack. "Reginald is a very good dog."

"I'm sure he is," said the woman, "but we had a problem with a dog earlier today — a very stinky one — so we aren't allowing any more dogs into the fair."

A stinky dog? Amy and Jack looked at each other, but they didn't say a word.

So Reginald was taken to the car where he waited for Amy and Jack to return. As soon as he was alone, Reginald jumped into the front seat and stared out the windshield.

He could see the twinkling lights of the fair and hear the merry-go-round music and the clickety-clack of the roller coaster.